Dear Parent:
Your child's love of reading starts here!

Every child learns to read in a different way and at his or her own speed. You can help your young reader improve and become more confident by encouraging his or her own interests and abilities. You can also guide your child's spiritual development by reading stories with biblical values and Bible stories, like I Can Read! books published by Zonderkidz. From books your child reads with you to the first books he or she reads alone, there are I Can Read! books for every stage of reading:

SHARED READING
Basic language, word repetition, and whimsical illustrations, ideal for sharing with your emergent reader.

BEGINNING READING
Short sentences, familiar words, and simple concepts for children eager to read on their own.

READING WITH HELP
Engaging stories, longer sentences, and language play for developing readers.

READING ALONE
Complex plots, challenging vocabulary, and high-interest topics for the independent reader.

ADVANCED READING
Short paragraphs, chapters, and exciting themes for the perfect bridge to chapter books.

I Can Read! books have introduced children to the joy of reading since 1957. Featuring award-winning authors and illustrators and a fabulous cast of beloved characters, I Can Read! books set the standard for beginning readers.

A lifetime of discovery begins with the magical words **"I Can Read!"**

Visit www.icanread.com for information on enriching your child's reading experience.
Visit www.zonderkidz.com for more Zonderkidz I Can Read! titles.

As a mother comforts her child,
I will comfort you.
—Isaiah 66:13

www.zonderkidz.com

Mommy, May I Hug the Fish?
ISBN-10: 0-310-71468-0
ISBN-13: 978-0-310-71468-2

Requests for information should be addressed to:
Zonderkidz, Grand Rapids, Michigan 49530

Library of Congress Cataloging-in-Publication Data

applied for

Art Direction: Jody Langley
Cover Design: Sarah Molegraaf

Printed in China

07 08 09 10 • 10 9 8 7 6 5 4 3 2 1

Mommy, May I Hug the Fish?

story by Crystal Bowman

pictures by Donna Christensen

"Mommy, may I hug the fish?
May I give the fish a kiss?"

Mommy says, “No, no, no.

You may look.

Do not touch.

Fish don’t like that very much.”

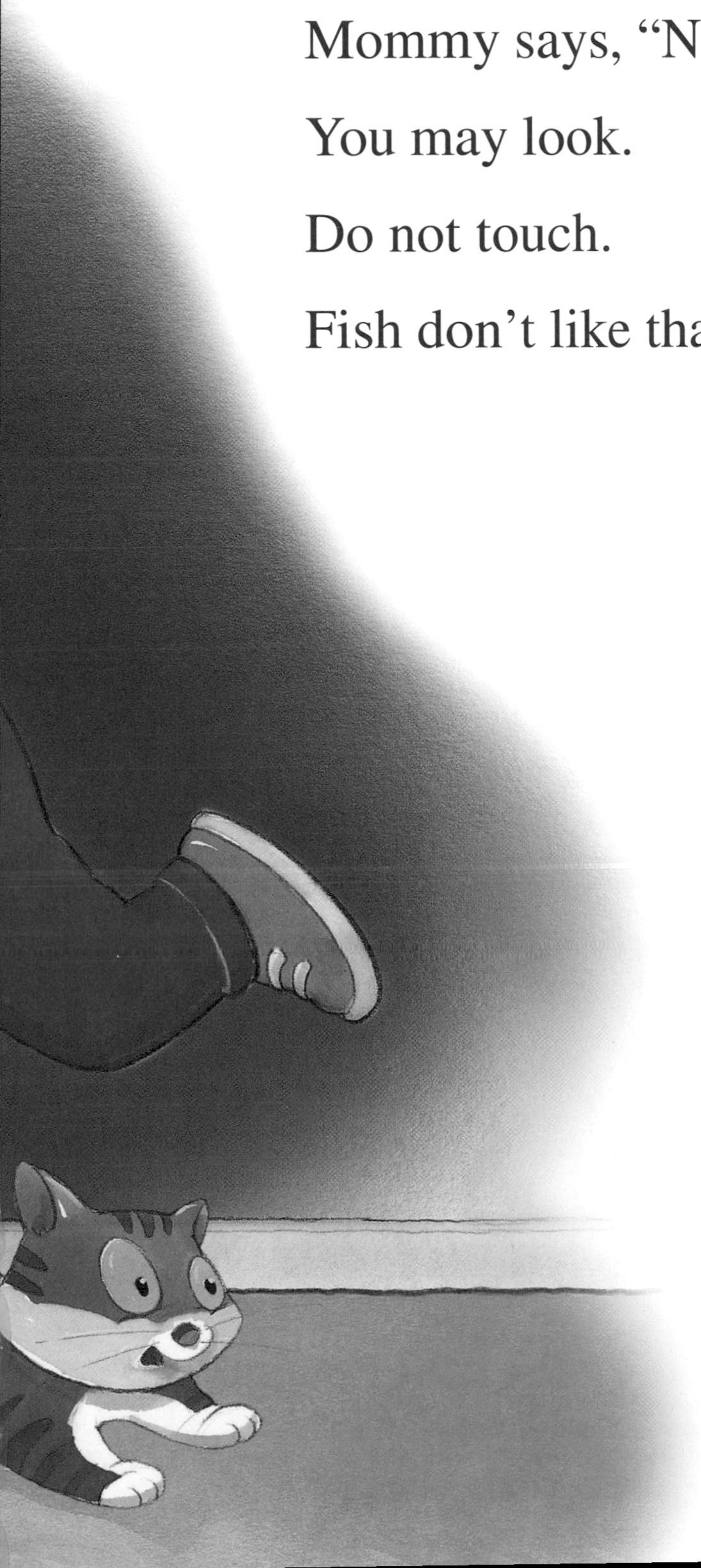

“Mommy, can we make a cake?
May I help you mix and bake?”

Mommy says, “Yes, yes, yes.
Here’s a bowl and flour too.
We will make a cake for you.”

"Mommy, may I turn the knob?

May I turn the oven on?"

Mommy says, “No, no, no.

The oven is hot,

so very hot!

No, my child, you may not.

I will have to turn the knob.

That is always Mommy's job."

“Mommy, may I play outside?
May I give my bear a ride?”

Mommy says, “Yes, yes, yes.

Give your teddy bear a ride.

Run and jump and play outside.”

"Mommy, may I use my feet
to walk alone
across the street?"

Mommy says, “No, no, no!

You may not go on your own.

It’s not safe to cross alone.

Hold my hand.

I'll walk with you.

That is what you need to do."

“Mommy, may I say a prayer?

Will God hear me?

Does he care?”

Mommy says, “Yes, yes, yes.

Tell him what you want to say.

God will hear you when you pray.

You can pray at noon or night.

Any time is always right."

"Mommy, may I sing and clap?

May I sit upon your lap?"

Mommy says, “Yes, yes, yes.

Let’s read a book.

Let’s sing and clap.

You may sit right in my lap.

You may take a little nap.”

Mommy says, “Shh, shh, shh.”